Drawing a Veil

Lari Don

A & C Black • London

The rights of Lari Don and Emma Chinnery to be identified
as the author and illustrator of this work have been asserted by them
in accordance with the Copyrights, Designs and Patents Act 1988.

ISBN 978-1-4081-5559-2

A CIP catalogue for this book is available from the British Library.

This book is produced using paper that is made from wood
grown in managed, sustainable forests. It is natural, renewable
and recyclable. The logging and manufacturing processes conform
to the environmental regulations of the country of origin.

Printed by CPI Group (UK), Croydon, CR0 4YY

recommended by

www.catchup.org

Catch Up is a not-for-profit charity
which aims to address the problem of
underachievement that has its roots in
literacy and numeracy difficulties.

Drawing
A Veil

This book is dedicated to every girl's right
to make her own choices.

Contents

Chapter One

Staring at Amina

Some Year 10 boys were fighting at the end of the corridor but, for once, no-one was looking at them.

Everyone was looking at Amina.

"Why didn't you *tell* me?" Ellie whispered. "I'm your best friend!"

Amina shook her head. "I didn't want you to talk me out of it."

Mr MacIver opened the door to the Art Room. "Come in quietly," he said, but no one moved. Everyone was still looking at Amina's scarf.

It wasn't a striped school scarf. It wasn't a woolly scarf like your gran might have knitted. It wasn't a trendy glittery scarf from the shopping centre.

Amina was wearing a tight black headscarf. It was pinned around her head, covering her hair, her ears and her neck.

Of course, everyone had seen women wearing headscarves before. But they had never seen Amina in a headscarf. Yesterday, Amina had had a ponytail swinging at the back of her head, just like every other girl in the class.

Amina walked into the Art Room. Ellie and the rest of the pupils came in after her.

Mr MacIver had put the tables and chairs in three rows around an empty stool in the middle. Everyone sat down.

"Today we're going to draw a portrait," said Mr MacIver. "Who would like to be our model?"

Three or four people put their hands up. Amina was one of them.

"Amina?" said Mr McIver. "Do you want to be the model today?"

"I may as well," said Amina. "Everyone is staring at me anyway!" She went to sit on the empty stool.

After fifteen minutes, Ellie had drawn Amina's body, but she couldn't draw her face.

Ellie knew Amina's face almost as well as her own. Amina had a slim nose, dark eyes and a wide mouth. Ellie had drawn Amina's face loads of times. But she had always drawn it with lots of long hair. Now she was trying to draw Amina's face in a frame of black scarf, with straight lines on each side.

Ellie gave up on her first drawing. She turned the paper over and started again. This time she drew Amina from memory.

Mr McIver stood behind her. He said, "That's a good drawing. But are you looking at your model?"

"This is what she looks like!" Ellie said.

Mr McIver laughed. "Look again."

Ellie looked up at her friend, then down at her picture. She had drawn Amina without the headscarf.

Chapter Two

Do Best Friends
Share Everything?

Ellie turned to Carlie, who was sitting
beside her, and asked if she could borrow her
rubber.

"Sure," said Carlie. "Why is Amina wearing that headscarf?"

Ellie looked hard at the drawing. Maybe she could turn some of the hair into scarf. She just had to rub out the wavy bits.

"I said," Carlie whispered, "why is Amina wearing that scarf?"

"How should I know?" Ellie said.

"Didn't she tell you?" asked Carlie. "I thought you were best friends now. I thought best friends shared *everything*! Remember, in the last year in primary school, you and I used to text each other about what *socks* we were going to wear, to make sure we always dressed the same."

Ellie blushed at the memory.

"Don't you know why she's wearing it?" asked Carlie.

"Of course I know," said Ellie. Really, she had no idea. "It's… em … it's to hide her hair from God. From Allah. It's her religion. Like not eating bacon. It's no big deal."

"No big deal?" snorted Carlie. "It's like she's wearing a big sign saying, 'Look at me, I'm different!'"

Ellie looked at her picture. There was Amina with a scarf on her head and a grey halo around it, where Ellie had rubbed out the hair.

"Yeah. Well," Ellie said. "She is different. We're all different. And it's her choice, isn't it?"

The door opened, and Megan and her sidekick Kate slid in.

"Sorry we're late, Mr Mac, the bus broke down," said Megan.

She walked round to her seat, and swung her bag off her shoulder, knocking Liam's pencil case onto the floor. Megan looked at it. Then she stood on it. Everyone heard it crunch, as pencils broke under her boot.

She grinned, then said, "Sorry, ginger," as Liam went bright red.

Kate giggled. "What are we drawing today?" she asked Liam.

But before Liam could answer, both girls looked up at the stool in the middle. Ellie saw Megan's pale face change as she saw Amina.

Megan looked for a long time at Amina's scarf, then she began to grin nastily.

Chapter Three

Mugshot

At the end of the double period of Art, Mr MacIver said, "Ellie, can you please collect the drawings, and put them on my desk? Everyone else, pack up."

Ellie walked round, picking up the sketches. Most of the pictures were pretty good, but Megan had scribbled two cartoons of Amina's head, one facing forward and one side on, like police photos of criminals. And under the cartoons Megan had written: 'Wanted: suicide bomber'.

Ellie put out her hand to pick up Megan's drawing but Megan pulled it out of reach. "This is for the notice-board."

Ellie dived across the desk and grabbed the paper. "You did it in Mr Mac's class, so he should mark it."

Megan tried to grab the picture back, but Ellie stepped behind Liam's chair.

Megan started to chase after Ellie, but Liam stood up and pushed his chair back to block Megan's way. Ellie put the pictures on the teacher's desk, with Megan's nasty cartoon right at the bottom.

As Ellie walked back to her seat, she heard Lauren, the quietest girl in the class, whisper to Amina, "You look really grown up and elegant in that scarf."

Once Ellie and Amina were alone in the classroom, Amina reached for her big purple bag. "Have you ever been the model for art class?" she asked Ellie. "It's quite weird. What were the pictures like?"

"They were a bit weird too," Ellie said, "because for some reason, everyone drew you with a headscarf on."

They walked into the empty corridor.

Ellie turned to Amina. "Why are you wearing a headscarf? And why didn't you *tell* me? I'm your best friend, and I didn't know. I looked like an idiot, standing there with my mouth open, when you turned up this morning in that… whatever it is."

"It's called hijab. And it's part of my religion," said Amina.

"Did your mum make you wear it?" asked Ellie.

"Have you ever seen my mum in hijab? She's not going to make me wear it when she doesn't wear it herself! It was my idea. I'm old enough to cover myself, so I'm wearing it to show my support for my sisters."

"You don't have any sisters," said Ellie. "You just have that great lump of a brother."

"I mean my Muslim sisters. All over the world," said Amina.

"Oh," said Ellie as she walked down the stairs. "So is it to stop your god seeing your hair?"

"My God, your god, anyone's god, can see whatever they like," said Amina. "No, I'm wearing it to show that I'm a modest Muslim woman."

"Modest?" Ellie laughed. "Modest! You always do a turn at the school talent show. You're not modest!"

"I don't have to be modest about my skills," Amina told her. "Just my body."

"You're not modest when you score at netball," said Ellie.

"I don't have to be modest about that either," said Amina. "It's about not wearing miniskirts or low-cut tops, about not *showing off* my body."

"What about fancy shoes?" Ellie asked, as Amina clicked down the stairs beside her in the highest heels she could get away with at school.

Amina laughed. "One step at a time!"

Chapter Four

What Is Normal Anyway?

After break, Amina had history and Ellie had science.

Ellie sat down in front of a row of test tube racks, and Carlie sat beside her.

"So? What did Amina say about the scarf?" asked Carlie.

Ellie sighed. "Like I told you. It's a religious thing. It's totally normal."

"Yeah. Normal for *her*. But what about you?"

"What about me?" asked Ellie.

"She won't want to pal around with you any more, will she?" said Carlie. "You don't believe in God. You're not going to wear a headscarf. How can you be her friend if you don't do the same as her? She'll want new friends. Maybe she'll go to a different school."

"No, she won't!" snapped Ellie.

"But she can't go to discos with that on, can she? You could come with me, though. Just like old times," said Carlie.

Miss Brown came in, and Carlie stopped talking. She scribbled a note and shoved it onto Ellie's folder.

Meet at 6 at the mall?
Late night shopping!

Ellie put the note in her pocket. She hung out with Amina most Thursday nights. But perhaps Carlie was right, perhaps the new scarf-wearing Amina wouldn't hang out any more.

At lunch, Ellie found Amina in the
canteen. They grabbed some sandwiches,
then went to the playground.

Ellie ate her lunch first. She needed the
energy to ask the question which had been
worrying her.

When she had finished her sandwich, she turned to Amina.

"What about me, then?" she asked. "Am I not modest because I'm not wearing a headscarf? Am I a loose woman?"

Amina looked at her carefully. Ellie looked down too. Pumps. Tights. Short skirt. Shorter cardigan.

Amina grinned. "You look like my best mate Ellie. And if you're happy like that, great. But I wasn't happy like that. I'm happy like this." She pointed to her longer cardigan, baggy trousers, and the dark scarf. "This is me standing up and saying I'm proud to be a Muslim..."

"STAND UP, YOU HORRIBLE LITTLE WORM!"

The roar of anger came from the wall by the car park.

Some Year 10 boys were gathered in a pack round a small red-haired boy.

The tallest Year 10 boy, Dale, shouted again. "You're sitting on our wall!"

There was a quiet answer, in a voice so squeaky it had to be a Year 7.

"That's Luke," said Amina. "Liam's little brother."

Dale turned to his mates. "What will we do with him?"

"Luke's got asthma," said Amina. "We can't let Dale batter him."

"I'll go and find Liam…" said Ellie.

But Amina said, "There's no time!" And she ran, on her stupid heels, straight towards the group of boys.

Ellie took a deep breath and ran after her.

Chapter Five

Musical Statues

Dale had already picked Luke up, and was shaking him.

Amina pushed Dale in the back. "Put him down. He didn't know it was your wall."

Dale swung Luke into Amina.

She stumbled back, and Ellie put a hand on Amina's shoulder to stop her falling to the ground. Amina said again, "Put him down! He's got asthma."

"Then he should be in the sick room. Maybe we should put *both* of you in the sick room," jeered Dale. He shoved Luke at one of his huge mates, and stepped towards Amina.

Ellie looked around and saw Mr MacIver walking into the car park. "Teacher!" she said loudly.

Dale stepped back. His mate dropped Luke. Amina pushed Luke away, and said, "Get out of here, quick." As Luke ran off, Dale grabbed Amina's arm.

Mr MacIver walked towards them. He had no idea what was going on. Teachers never do.

Dale and Amina looked like they were chatting, or even flirting. But really Dale was gripping her arm too tightly for her to get away. They all stood as if they were playing a game of musical statues. No-one would move or speak until the teacher walked past.

Ellie broke the rules, and the spell. "Mr MacIver!"

"Yes?" He stopped and smiled at her.

"Amina didn't see her portraits this morning," said Ellie. "Could she see them now?"

"Of course," said Mr MacIver. "Come and have a quick look, before the bell goes."

Mr MacIver watched Amina and Ellie step away from the boys, then he turned towards the school, and the girls walked safely beside him.

They didn't get a chance to talk on their own while they were looking at the drawings, then they had to dash to their classes. English for Ellie, PE for Amina.

"See you tonight?" asked Amina as she ran towards the gym. "Usual time, usual place?"

Ellie didn't nod. She still had Carlie's note in her pocket. Carlie didn't stand out in the crowd. Carlie didn't stand up to bullies. Carlie didn't make Ellie ask herself hard questions.

Chapter Six

Hard Questions

Ellie left the house at 5.30, which gave her plenty of time to walk to the park, or get a bus to the shops for six o'clock.

She still hadn't decided where she was going.

She wasn't wearing a hat. Or a hood. Or a scarf. It was a nice night. There was no need to cover up. It was just daft.

What did 'being modest' mean, anyway? Was Amina saying if you didn't cover yourself then you were showing off, or asking for trouble?

And this standing up and being a Muslim thing. Where had that come from? Amir and Yusuf prayed every lunchtime. Amina never did.

Ellie decided to go to the park first, to see if Amina was still wearing that scarf. She could always meet Carlie later.

She walked towards the kids' play park, where she usually met Amina. They didn't climb the rope frame or use the slide any more, but there were swings to sit on and trees to block the wind off the sea. Behind the fence some boys were having a kick-about.

She saw Amina pushing herself on a swing. Amina was wearing jeans, a long coat, and seriously high purple heels. She wasn't wearing the black headscarf.

Instead, she was wearing a purple and gold headscarf. It went with her shoes, and the big bag on the ground.

Oh great, thought Ellie. *She's got a whole wardrobe of headscarves.*

She stopped, halfway between the bus stop and the swings. She couldn't decide which way to go.

Amina saw her and waved. Ellie waved back, and walked over to her.

"I thought wearing a headscarf was about supporting your Muslim sisters," Ellie said.

"It is. Why?" Amina asked.

Ellie sat on the other swing. "Well, if you want to show everyone at school that you're standing up with your Muslim sisters, I can understand that. But you don't have to do it when you're hanging out with me, do you? Can't you take it off just now?"

"No, Ellie. It's not a part-time thing. It's my life."

Ellie twisted round and round on the swing. She didn't know what to say next.

Chapter Seven

Driving Boys Wild

"Oi! Al-Qaeda babe!" It was Megan's voice.

Megan and Kate stepped out from behind the slide. Amina and Ellie jumped off the swings.

"Having a bad hair day, Amina?" asked Megan. "Or have you got nits?"

"What's in the bag, Amina? A bomb?" Kate kicked Amina's bag.

"Don't kick it, idiot," said Megan. "It might explode."

Megan stepped right up to Amina. "If we take this off, do you shrivel up and die? Or do you drive boys wild with your beauty?" She tugged at the scarf.

Amina shoved Megan's hand away. Ellie moved round Kate to get Amina's bag.

"Are you leaving, Ellie?" asked Megan. "Quite right. She might cover you in veils, then marry you to someone you've never met."

"Hey, don't knock it," said Amina. "If you want to get married, you'll *need* to find someone who's never met you, or seen your face. Anyone else would run a mile."

Megan gave a yell of rage and hit out at Amina. Ellie swung Amina's bag at the back of Megan's knees. Megan fell over, knocking into Kate. Ellie chucked Amina her bag, then they ran through the gate towards home.

Megan yelled, "Stop them! Stop the terrorists!"

Just ahead of Ellie and Amina were the boys playing football. They turned round to stare at the running girls.

Then Ellie saw who the boys were.

Megan was still screeching, "Stop them!"

And Dale, with the football at his feet, smiled.

Ellie and Amina were caught between Megan and Kate behind and Dale and his mates in front.

The girls swerved left onto the grass, and headed for the nearest road.

"Pull her scarf off!" screamed Megan.

Dale yelled back, "We'll catch her, and you can have the scarf!"

Ellie was in flat boots, and Amina was in her daft high heels. But Amina was much better at PE, so they ran at the same pace as they sprinted out of the park.

They turned the corner and headed for the harbour.

"We could hide up a side street," panted Amina, but they heard shouts as Megan, Kate and the boys turned the corner behind them. They couldn't hide yet. They had to keep going.

Chapter Eight

Running, Together

They reached a busy crossing as the lights turned green. The traffic started moving, but there were half a dozen boys behind them with their blood high and their brains turned off.

Ellie stopped at the kerb, but Amina grabbed her hand and pulled her onto the road.

They dodged between cars, banging past bumpers, and scraping along doors.

The exhaust fumes made them cough, and burned their legs.

They leapt onto the pavement, and kept running, still holding hands.

Ellie glanced back. A bus had stopped between them and the gang behind them, so no-one saw them as they swerved into an alley.

They came out at the docks. There were dirty cargo ships to their right, and the white shopping centre was ahead. Ellie wondered if Carlie was having fun in there.

They looked back. No-one was chasing them down the alley.

"Keep going," gasped Amina.

They were crossing the bridge over the dirty city river when they heard a distant shout.

"Over the rail," panted Ellie. They climbed on to the iron railings then scrambled to the girders on the underside of the bridge.

Ellie nearly lost her balance and Amina reached over to steady her. There was a splash.

Amina whispered, "Oops. I lost a shoe."

They crouched under the bridge and listened, but they didn't hear shouts or running footsteps.

It was a long time before Amina and Ellie felt it was safe to talk.

"What will you do at school?" Ellie asked. "Megan and Dale are *both* after you now."

"They're after you too. Sorry. But don't worry. Megan will find someone else to pick on soon. And those boys have the attention spans of goldfish, they'll have forgotten us by Monday."

"But we still have to get through tomorrow. How will we do that?" Ellie said.

"Maybe we should go in disguise?" Amina suggested. "I've got some scarves you could borrow."

There was a short silence. Then Ellie giggled. "I don't think they'd suit me!"

They climbed out from under the bridge as darkness fell.

Once they were on the pavement, Ellie looked at Amina's feet. "Can you walk with just one shoe?"

"I've still got my trainers in my bag from PE," said Amina.

"Did you wear the scarf for PE?" Ellie asked.

"Yeah. And it got in the way every time I tried to score!"

Ellie laughed. "You'll get used to it. We all will."

Amina pulled her trainers on, and chucked the single high heel over the rail into the water. She nodded. "Everyone will get used to it."

Dead Wood

Holly's family move to the old house so
her dad can do his job: bulldozing the ancient
trees to make way for a housing estate. But
there's something haunting the old house.
Something old, and angry, that doesn't want
the trees cut down. Something *alive*...

ISBN 978-1-4081-6335-1
RRP £5.99

Zero to Hero

Will is football mad, but he's the shortest boy in the year, and one of the slowest. He knows his skills at passing and ball control could make up for his lack of size, but the team coach is looking for fast players. Will he ever get a chance to show what he can do?

ISBN 978-1-4081-5560-8
RRP £5.99

Pitch Dark

David wants to be on the school team, like he was before. But Nick, the current goalie, has killed off any hope of that. Walking home one night, David meets a stranger who will change his life forever. But will David's football dream turn into a living nightmare?

ISBN 978-1-4081-5573-8
RRP £5.99